First published in Great Britain in 2006
By W.F Graham (Northampton) Ltd
for Lomond Books Ltd, Broxburn, EH52 5NF

Text © John Abernethy
© Lomond Books Ltd, 2006
www.lomondbooks.com

ISBN 1-842-04086-3

In the Highlands of Scotland on the banks of Loch In Roull, at the foot of the mountain Beinn Aigh Hill, there is a village by the name of Dunguid. In the village there was a shop, a post office, a hotel, a church, a school and a herd of twenty-two Highland cows.
The youngest cow was a calf called Heather.

Heather had lived all her life in Dunguid and loved to stroll around the village. She would go from the top field at one end to the bottom field at the other, saying hello to the villagers and tourists as she went.

Dunguid could be a sleepy place and on one hot summers day Heather felt very sleepy indeed. She went down to the shore and found a pleasant spot in the shade of a tree to watch the birds and the boats on the still blue water. Before long, Heather was fast asleep.

When Heather awoke, Duncan the oyster-catcher was standing next to her.
"Did you have a good sleep Heather?" said Duncan
"I think I slept too long!" said Heather
"My family will be wondering where I am."
"Can you swim?" asked Duncan
"No" said Heather, "Why do you ask?"
"You will soon find out!" said Duncan and flew off.

"How peculiar!" thought Heather. She looked out into the loch and saw a seal waving at her. "Hello, I'm Heather" said Heather.
"Hello Heather, I'm Jake." said the seal. "Are you lost?"
Heather shook her head.

"Can you swim?" asked Jake
"No!' said Heather "Why do you ask?"
"Go back to the village and you will soon find out!" said Jake who gave
a cheery wave and swam away.

"How strange!" thought Heather. Everyone was acting so oddly! With a sigh, Heather decided to go back to the village. She turned round and would you believe it - the path to the village was no longer there! No, path, no beach, just water everywhere!

Heather was confused. She walked to her left and
walked to her right and everywhere she looked there was water! She
was on an island! How on earth had that happened?

She looked across to the village. On the street of the village looking
back at her, were all the other cows and all the villagers.
"Oh no!" thought Heather, "I'm in trouble now!"

"Are you lost?" said a deep voice next to Heather.
She turned round, and sitting on the small island was a polar bear,
wearing sunglasses and a red sunhat, sipping a glass of lemonade!
Heather was suprised! She had never seen a polar bear before!

"My name is Conrad." said the polar bear.
"I am from Canada and am on holiday in Dunguid."
"I'm Heather. Are you having a nice holiday?" Heather asked, as it was best to be polite to visitors.

"Excellent, excellent!" said Conrad. "But what about you? How are you going to get back to the village? Can you swim?"
Heather shook her head. She felt very sad. She was stuck on an island with a Canadian polar bear called Conrad, with everyone she knew watching her from the village!

"I know what we will do!" said Conrad, "We will catch a boat!" And with that, Conrad shouted in the loudest voice Heather had ever heard; "BOAT, BOAT, BOAT, BOAT!"

At first the villagers were baffled as to why the polar bear was shouting in such a loud voice. Then they realised that Conrad wanted them to send a boat to take Heather back to the village!

Morag was the best sailor in Dunguid and she took her boat "The Serena" to the island. Heather stepped into the boat and Morag sailed back to shore. All the villagers cheered and all the cows mooed!

When Heather got back to the village, everyone decided to go to the hotel to celebrate. There was music and dancing and drinks and pizza and chips. Conrad stayed on the island and gave Heather a wave.

The following day, Heather came back to the village with the herd. When she looked out at the loch the island was gone! The tree was still there, but there was no water!

"Where has the island gone?" Heather asked Crawford, her Dad.
"It's the tide!" explained Crawford. "In the morning the tide goes out and in the afternoon the water comes in and your island will be there again!"

"But where has Conrad gone?" asked Heather.
"On his way back to Canada." said Crawford
Heather felt sad.
"Conrad left you a present." said Crawford and pointed to the tree.
Next to the tree was Conrad's red sunhat.